Life Cycles
Butterflies and Moths

Julie K. Lundgren

ROURKE
PUBLISHING

www.rourkepublishing.com

www.rourkepublishing.com

Photo credits: Cover © Mau Horng, Chris Turner, Lori Skelton, Kati Molin; Title Page © Kati Molin; Contents © Luna Vandoorne, Cathy Keifer, EtiAmmos; Page 4 © Chekaramit; Page 5 © Ambient Ideas; Page 6 © Elizabeth Spencer; Page 7 © Chekaramit, Louis Bourgeois; Page 8 © Maryunin Yury Vasilevich; Page 9 © limpid; Page 10 © Mau Horng; Page 11 © Luna Vandoorne; Page 12/13 © Cathy Keifer; Page 14 © Ianaré Sévi; Page 15 © Dr. Morley Read, Chekaramit; Page 16 © Andy Heyward; Page 17 © Cathy Keifer, EtiAmmos; Page 18 © Jens Stolt, Yenyu Shih, Michael C. Gray; Page 19 © Laurie Barr; Page 21 © nikkytok, Ambient Ideas; Page 22 © Luna Vandoorne, Cathy Keifer, Andy Heyward, limpid

Editor: Jeanne Sturm

Cover and page design by Nicola Stratford, bdpublishing.com

Library of Congress Cataloging-in-Publication Data

Lundgren, Julie K.
 Butterflies and moths / Julie K. Lundgren.
   p. cm. -- (Life cycles)
 Includes bibliographical references and index.
 ISBN 978-1-61590-308-5 (Hard Cover) (alk. paper)
 ISBN 978-1-61590-547-8 (Soft Cover)
 1. Butterflies--Life cycles--Juvenile literature. 2. Moths--Life cycles--Juvenile literature. I. Title.
 QL544.2.L86 2011
 595.78'9--dc22
                              2010009024

Rourke Publishing
Printed in the United States of America, North Mankato, Minnesota
033010
033010LP

www.rourkepublishing.com - rourke@rourkepublishing.com
Post Office Box 643328, Vero Beach, Florida 32964

Table of Contents

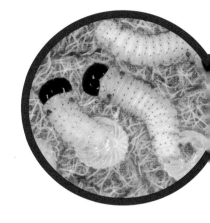

Insect Beauties

Butterflies and moths belong to the insect group of animals. They have bodies divided into three sections called the head, **thorax**, and **abdomen**. The head has eyes and **antennae**. Wings and feet attach to the thorax.

Hawk moth

Like most other insects, butterflies and moths have six legs and two pairs of wings.

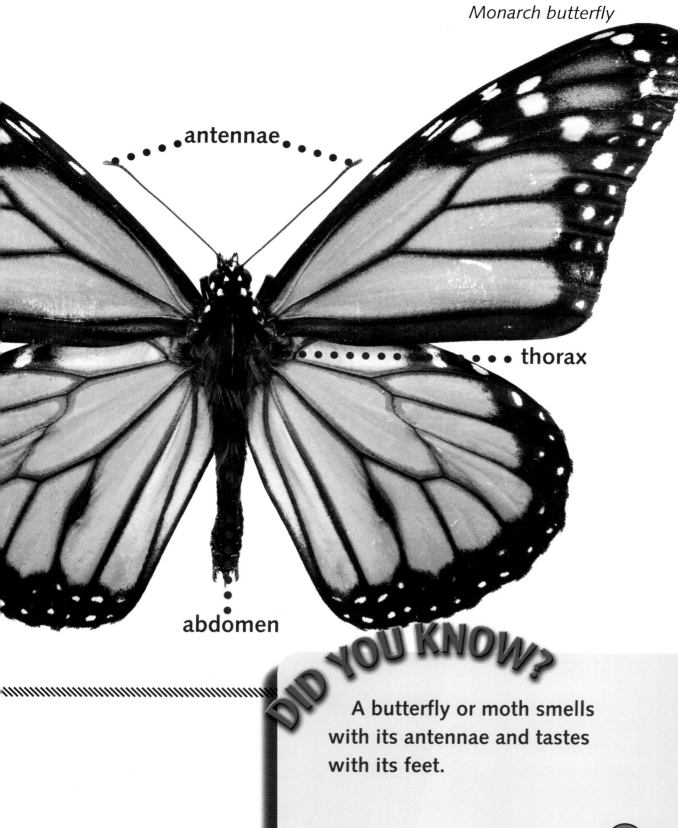

Monarch butterfly

antennae

thorax

abdomen

DID YOU KNOW?

A butterfly or moth smells with its antennae and tastes with its feet.

Butterflies and moths differ in several ways.

	Moth	**Butterfly**
Antennae	Simple or fuzzy, no clubs	Usually plain, with clubbed ends
Most active time of day	Dawn, dusk, or night	Day
Wing Position at Rest	Flat, open	Straight up, together
Colors	Usually dull, with patterns that help them blend in	Colorful, with bold patterns
Body Shape	Chunkier	Slender

Moth antennae can be straight or feathery, but have no end clubs.

Blood-vein moth

6

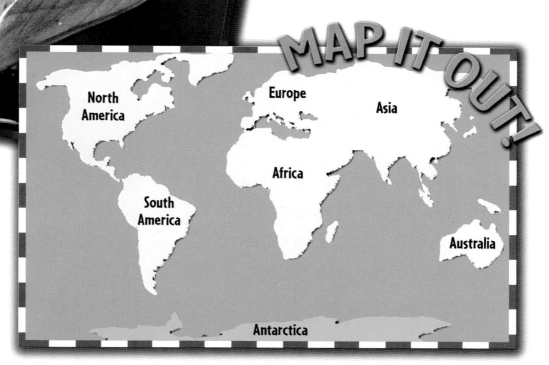

North America

Europe

Asia

Africa

South America

Australia

Antarctica

Butterflies and moths live on every continent but Antarctica.

Butterfly antennae have little clubs, or bumps, on the ends.

Monarch butterfly

DID YOU KNOW?

Scientists think 12,000 to 15,000 kinds of butterflies and 150,000 to 250,000 kinds of moths live on Earth. More await discovery!

Butterflies and moths feed other animals. They **pollinate** flowers so plants can make seeds. They give people an idea about habitat health, too. If the habitat is too polluted, butterflies and moths leave or die.

A dark clouded yellow butterfly finds a tasty lunch inside a knautia flower.

Many flowers depend on butterflies, like this common jay butterfly, for pollination.

Egg-cellent Start

All living things have a life cycle. They begin life, grow, **reproduce**, and then die. The cycle happens again and again. Insects like butterflies and moths change forms as they go through their life cycle. They begin as tiny eggs.

Butterflies and moths may lay round, oval, bumpy, smooth, or striped eggs. Each kind of butterfly or moth lays eggs with a particular shape, color, and pattern.

Depending on the kind, butterflies and moths may lay many eggs together or just one egg on each plant or leaf.

DID YOU KNOW?

Butterflies and moths lay eggs on plants their caterpillars like to eat. Monarchs lay eggs on milkweed.

Eating Machines

After 3 to 10 days, the eggs hatch and the second stage of life begins. A caterpillar, or larva, grows quickly. It sheds its skin, or molts, when its skin gets too tight. Caterpillars molt several times.

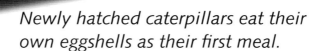

Newly hatched caterpillars eat their own eggshells as their first meal.

New skin gives the monarch caterpillars growing room.

The time between each molt is called an instar. Monarch butterflies have five instars.

13

Animals enjoy eating caterpillars. How do any survive? Color forms one defense. Bold colors and patterns often signal a warning that the caterpillars contain poison. Green caterpillars blend into their surroundings.

Caterpillars eat night and day. Their bodies store the energy they get from food. They must gather enough energy for the changes to come.

Some caterpillars, like the giant swallowtail, look like lumps of bird droppings.

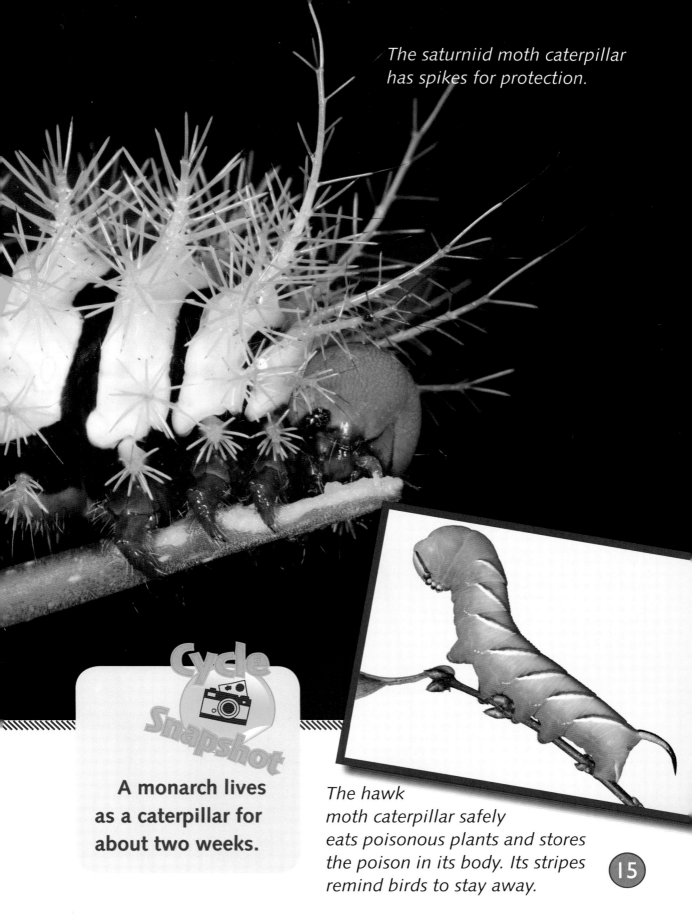

The saturniid moth caterpillar has spikes for protection.

Cycle Snapshot

A monarch lives as a caterpillar for about two weeks.

The hawk moth caterpillar safely eats poisonous plants and stores the poison in its body. Its stripes remind birds to stay away.

Changes

Fully grown caterpillars search for a safe place to begin the **pupa** stage. After attaching their tails to a branch or leaf, butterfly caterpillars molt one last time, revealing the **chrysalis**. Many moths spin silk **cocoons** around themselves. Others form a hard shell and rest on the ground.

The monarch butterfly forms a chrysalis that looks like hanging fruit.

The monarch caterpillar forms its chrysalis in several steps, beginning with a hook that looks like the letter J.

DID YOU KNOW?

An Atlas Moth has wings 10 to 12 inches (25 to 30 centimeters) from tip to tip.

Many kinds of moth caterpillars, like lappet moths, form cocoons in which to change to adults.

Inside the chrysalis or cocoon, the caterpillar's body changes. Much of it breaks down into a rich soup that provides food for the developing adult.

After the chrysalis breaks open, the new butterfly rests several hours. It must dry its wet wings before it can fly.

Chrysalises come in many colors and patterns.

A monarch butterfly spends about 12-14 days in its chrysalis before coming out as an adult butterfly.

Wonderful Wings

Many butterflies and moths sip flower nectar for energy; while others dine on moist, rotting fruit, tree sap, or animal waste. They find partners and lay eggs to begin the life cycle again. Near summer's end, some kinds **migrate** to warm wintering grounds.

Zoos and nature centers often plant gardens especially for butterflies and moths. The gardens contain flowering plants that butterflies, moths, and their caterpillars like. Plant a few favorites in your yard!

Cycle Snapshot

Female butterflies and moths lay several hundred eggs in their lifetime. Few become adults, as little as one or two out of every 100 eggs laid.

Blue morpho butterflies, like other adult butterflies, cannot chew. They drink their food instead.

DID YOU KNOW?

Monarch butterflies migrate south in the fall. Monarchs return each spring to lay eggs.

Life Cycle Round-up

1 Butterflies and moths begin as eggs.

4 Adults come out to begin the cycle again.

3 It then forms a chrysalis or cocoon.

2 A caterpillar, or larva, hatches, eats, grows, and molts several times.

Glossary

abdomen (AB-duh-muhn): the last section of an insect, behind the thorax

antennae (an-TEN-ay): the two parts on the head of a butterfly or moth that sense smells

chrysalis (KRISS-uh-liss): the special protective shell in which a butterfly pupa changes to an adult

cocoons (KAH-koonz): the woven, protective coverings in which moth caterpillars change to adults

migrate (MYE-grate): move from one area to another according to the seasons

pollinate (POL-uh-nate): move plant pollen from one flower to another, allowing seeds to develop

pupa (PYOO-puh): the stage of development between a caterpillar and an adult

reproduce (ree-proh-DOOS): make more of something

thorax (THOR-aks): the body section located between the head and abdomen

Index

Websites to Visit

www.butterfliesandmoths.org/

www.flmnh.ufl.edu/butterflies/

www.kidsbutterfly.org/

www.fs.fed.us/monarchbutterfly/index.shtml

www.monarchwatch.org/biology/cycle1.htm

www.thebutterflysite.com/

About the Author

Julie K. Lundgren grew up near Lake Superior where she reveled in mucking about in the woods, picking berries, and expanding her rock collection. Her appetite for learning about nature led her to a degree in biology from the University of Minnesota. She currently lives in Minnesota with her husband and two sons.